壮族神话传说少儿绘本

The Magical Bird－Feather Costume

百鸟衣

编著：南宁市博物馆 / 广西霖创文化创意有限责任公司

广西美术出版社
GUANGXI FINE ARTS PUBLISHING HOUSE

图书在版编目（CIP）数据

百鸟衣：中文、英文 / 南宁市博物馆，广西霖创文化创
意有限责任公司编著. —南宁：广西美术出版社，2020.12
（壮族神话传说少儿绘本）
ISBN 978-7-5494-2278-4

Ⅰ . ①百… Ⅱ . ①南… ②广… Ⅲ . ①儿童文学 - 图画故
事 - 中国 - 当代 Ⅳ . ①I287.8

中国版本图书馆CIP数据核字（2020）第234440号

百鸟衣 壮族神话传说少儿绘本

BAI NIAO YI ZHUANGZU SHENHUA CHUANSHUO SHAO' ER HUIBEN

编　　著：南宁市博物馆　广西霖创文化创意有限责任公司
主　　编：张晓剑 / 覃　忠 / 周佳璐
编　　委：刘德雨 / 吕虹霖 / 蓝　涛 / 潘昕昊 / 欧　文 / 彭　柯
　　　　　梁　晨 / 咸　安 / 夏丽娜 / 黎琼泽 / 张沥仁 / 周　怡
绘　　画：周佳璐 / 张云浩 / 王恩惠 / 冯　磊 / 李　琼
英文译者：姚小文
英文审校：[英] Judith Sovin

出　版　人：陈　明
终　　　审：邓　欣
策 划 编 辑：谭　宇
责 任 编 辑：黄　玲　谭　宇
装 帧 设 计：谭　宇
校　　　对：梁冬梅
审　　　读：肖丽新
出 版 发 行：广西美术出版社
地　　　址：广西南宁市望园路9号（邮编：530023）
网　　　址：www.gxfinearts.com
印　　　刷：广西壮族自治区地质印刷厂
版 次 印 次：2020年12月第1版第1次印刷
开　　　本：889mm×1194mm　1/16
印　　　张：2
字　　　数：20千字
书　　　号：ISBN 978-7-5494-2278-4
定　　　价：45.00元

从前，三省坡上住着一个青年名叫

张亚原。

On Sansheng Slope lived a lad named

Zhang Yayuan.

他家境贫寒，从小就上山砍柴、打猎，练就了一身好本领。

Yayuan was born into a poor family, but he managed to learn many skills through cutting firewood and going hunting in the mountains.

夏日的一天，张亚原来到清水潭边，
躺在木棉树下小憩。

One day in summer, Yayuan came to
the Crystal Pool for a nap under a
bombax tree.

沉睡间，他梦见一个人面鸟身的人向他飞来。

Whilst he slept, Yayuan dreamt that a magical creature flew towards him. It had the body of a bird and the head of a human.

人面鸟身的人说，第二天正午会有一黑一黄两只鸟在空中搏斗，请张亚原射死黑鸟，救那只黄鸟。

The magical creature told him that two birds would appear fighting in the sky at midday the next day. One would be yellow and the other black. The magical creature asked him to shoot the black one and to save the yellow.

张亚原一觉醒来，觉得这个梦离奇古怪，
于是半信半疑地回家了。

第二天，他像往常一样上山打猎。

When he awoke, Yayuan pondered the
strange dream,
He made his way home, mulling over the
possible meaning.
The following day, he went hunting as usual.

正午时分，果然如昨天梦中场景一般，有两只鸟在空中搏斗！这是一场激烈的搏斗，黄鸟拼命地想从凶猛的黑鸟手中挣脱。

Exactly as his dream foretold: two birds appeared fighting in the sky at midday! The battle was fierce and it was hard for the yellow bird to escape.

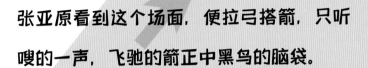

张亚原看到这个场面，便拉弓搭箭，只听嗖的一声，飞驰的箭正中黑鸟的脑袋。

As quick as a flash, Yayuan reached for his bow and arrow, and shot the black bird straight through.

黑鸟脖子一歪，栽进深谷去了。
被救下的黄鸟十分感激张亚原的
救命之恩。

The black bird fell from the sky
and plunged into a deep valley. The
yellow bird was extremely grateful
to Yayuan for his deeds.

它每天来到清水潭边，站在木棉树上，用优美动听的歌声娓娓唱出自己的爱慕之情。

From that day on, the yellow bird came to sit on the bombax tree by the Crystal Pool. It sang sweet love songs.

日子久了，黄鸟竟幻化成一个美丽的姑娘出现在张亚原面前，对他说道："救命恩人，我就是那只黄鸟，要是你不嫌弃，我愿与阿哥结为夫妻。"

Sometime later, the yellow bird magically transformed into a beautiful young woman! She spoke to Yayuan, "My dearest saviour, I am the yellow bird and I would like to be your wife."

勇敢善良的张亚原与美丽勤劳的黄鸟姑娘结为了夫妻，过着美好幸福的生活。

Yayuan was brave and kind. The young woman was beautiful and industrious. They loved each other, so they got married and lived happily together.

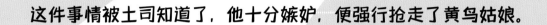

这件事情被土司知道了，他十分嫉妒，便强行抢走了黄鸟姑娘。

Nearby there lived an evil chieftain. He knew about the marriage of Yayuan and his beautiful wife. He was very jealous and decided to take the woman away.

临别时，黄鸟姑娘告诉张亚原，到山上射一百只鸟，用它们的羽毛制成"百鸟衣"，第一百天穿上"百鸟衣"去衙门里找她。黄鸟姑娘被抢进衙门后，她不再欢笑，变得十分忧伤。

Before she was abducted, the woman asked Yayuan to shoot one hundred birds to make a feather costume, and for him to wear it to the chieftain's mansion on the 100th day of their separation. The poor woman was held prisoner and became extremely sad.

张亚原为了救妻子，
蹚过了九十九条河，
爬过了九十九座山，
射落了一百只鸟。

Yayuan was determined to save his wife.
He waded through ninety-nine rivers and
climbed ninety-nine mountains on his quest
to shoot one hundred birds.

第一百天，张亚原终于做成了神奇的"百鸟衣"。

他将"百鸟衣"穿在身上，来到了衙门。

见到张亚原舞动着"百鸟衣"，

平日里满面愁容的黄鸟姑娘立刻露出了笑容。

On the 100th day, Yayuan completed his magical bird-feather costume and set off to rescue his wife. Finally, Yayuan arrived at the chieftain's mansion. The young woman smiled instantly at the sight of her husband flapping his wings in his fabulous costume.

愚蠢的土司贪婪"百鸟衣"的魔力，为了讨得黄鸟姑娘的欢心，便脱下官袍与张亚原换穿。

The chieftain was jealous of Yayuan's magical costume and craved it for himself. In order to possess the costume and win the heart of the beautiful woman, the chieftain stripped off his official robes and dressed himself in Yayuan's feather costume.

张亚原趁帮土司穿"百鸟衣"时杀死了土司。

Whilst helping the chieftain to put on
the costume, Yayuan took the chance to
kill the bad man.

张亚原救出了黄鸟姑娘,夺取了骏马,带着他心爱的妻子逃出了衙门,策马扬长而去。

Yayuan rescued his wife. They took the chieftain's best horse and rode away.

张亚原和他心爱的黄鸟姑娘一起奔赴自由、美好的未来。

Yayuan and his beloved wife lived happily ever after.